I Speak Peace

FERNE PRESS

D1307415

Written by Kate Carroll
Illustrated by Rainer M. Osinger

I Speak Peace

Layout and cover design by Jacqueline L. Challiss Hill
Illustrations created by Rainer M. Osinger
Illustrations created with watercolor

Printed in the United States of America

Summary: A delightful story that teaches readers how peace can make a positive impact in their lives.

Library of Congress Cataloging-in-Publication Data
Carroll, Kate
I Speak Peace/Kate Carroll–First Edition
ISBN-13: 978-1-938326-46-2
1. Peace. 2. Juvenile fiction. 3. Feelings.
I. Carroll, Kate II. Title
Library of Congress Control Number: 2016931026

FERNE PRESS

Ferne Press is an imprint of Nelson Publishing & Marketing
366 Welch Road, Northville, MI 48167
www.nelsonpublishingandmarketing.com
(248) 735-0418

Dedication

I dedicate this book to all of my students along the way. You have all been my inspiration and have brought me so much happiness and love throughout the years. You have demonstrated that with love, modeling, and patience, all children can be taught peace. I would especially like to mention my 2014–2015 and my 2015–2016 first-grade classes, who were along with me for this new journey. Thank you for your enthusiasm for this book and for embracing this message—speaking peace and making a positive difference in the world. I am so proud of all my little peacemakers as you continue to spread peace wherever you go.

First and foremost, I would like to give thanks to my parents, who have given me endless support and encouragement to help make this dream come true. I couldn't have done this without you. You have always been a tremendous source of inspiration, love, and strength. Thank you for being wonderful role models and raising me with love, instilling a strong faith in God, and teaching me the value and importance of peace. Thank you for always encouraging me to believe in myself and go after my dreams.

I would also like to acknowledge my closest friends and family for your support and encouragement. Thank you for always listening to all of the updates and ideas and for offering your opinions along the way. Your enthusiasm helped push me along.

I greatly appreciate the hard work of Rainer M. Osinger. Thank you so much for bringing the text to life with your delightful illustrations.

Lastly, many thanks to Marian Nelson and Kris Yankee for helping me make this book a reality and for believing in my message. Your guidance and support have been tremendously appreciated and valued. Thank you for helping me get this peaceful message out into the world so that together, we can all make a positive difference.

Peace.
What does that word mean?

Peace is a feeling we have when we are calm and happy.
Peace is how we express ourselves when we are loving and kind.
Peace is something we are when we are respectful and tolerant of others.

Peace is being free from violence and hatred.
Peace is working together to make the world a better place to live.

Peace begins within us-in our hearts and in our minds.
Peace within is finding the time to be quiet and calm.
And being content and thankful for the good in our lives.

It is letting go of angry thoughts, breathing them out.
And letting in happy thoughts, breathing them in.

Once we have peace within,
then we are ready to share
it with the world.

Our world is filled with all kinds of people.
We are all different in many ways
and even speak different languages.

But if you look closely, you will see that
we are more the same
than we are different.

We all have feelings.
We all need love and want to be happy.
We all need friends and families.

We all live on the same planet. We are all in charge of taking care of it . . .
and each other.
We are all part of one race . . . the human race.
And we all need to work together to make our world a more peaceful place.

Sometimes working together can be hard because we think we can't communicate or understand each other.

But we can.

There is one language we can all speak and understand . . .

peace.

We speak peace
when we treat others with
kindness and lend
a helping hand . . .

and when we tell others that we care about them.

We speak peace when we use our words
instead of our fists . . .

and when we work together toward a common goal.

We speak peace when we respect each other's differences . . .

and when we stand up for someone who needs our help.

We are speaking peace when we share in someone else's happiness or sorrow . . .

and when we forgive.

We don't even need to use words to speak peace.
We speak peace when we smile at someone . . .

and when we listen and share.

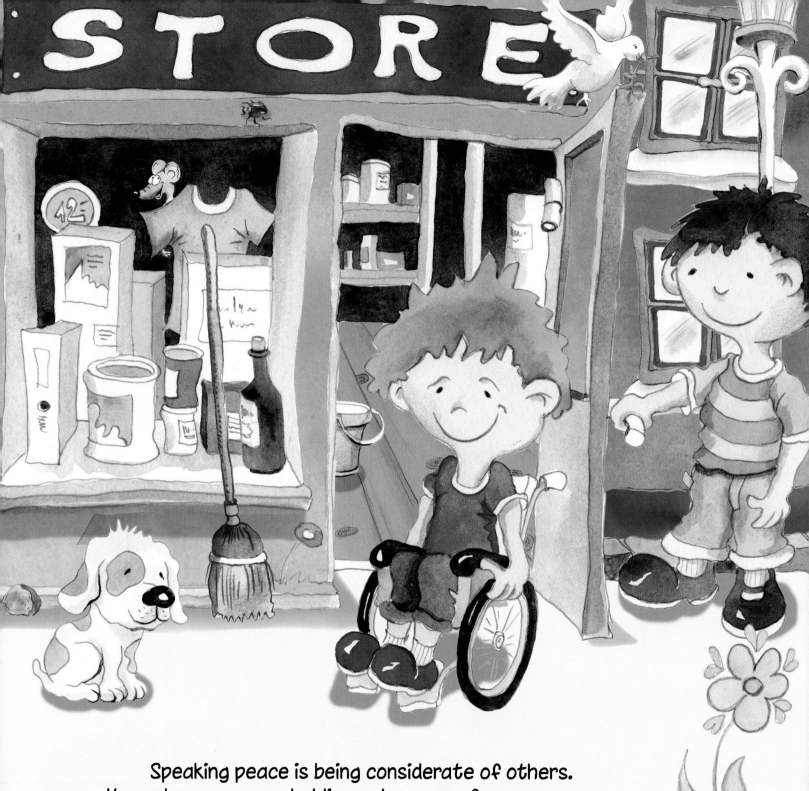

Speaking peace is being considerate of others.
It can be as easy as holding a door open for someone . . .

or giving a hug or a handshake.

We also speak peace when we are patient and understanding.

The more you speak peace, the easier it is! And the more you do it,
the more you will feel your heart filling with peace and happiness.
Speaking peace is contagious and will spread wide and far
like a dandelion in the wind.

You will see that even though we may be different in some ways, everyone all over the world can speak one language . . . peace. Imagine what our world would be like if we ALL speak peace! I speak peace.

Will you speak peace with me?

At a time when our world is in such strife and at an all-time high for violence, I felt the call to write a book that promotes peace and respect. I have taught peace in my classroom for many years and have seen the incredible, positive difference it makes in children and in our classroom. Now it's time to go beyond the walls of a classroom and spread peace into our homes, our communities, our countries, and all over the world. And, most importantly, into our hearts.

Now is the time for peace. Now is the time to create peacemakers. We have the power to bring peace to our world through the hope of our children, but we must teach it and we must speak it. Children are not born hating. They are not born prejudiced or racist. Those are things that are learned. Our children are born blank slates, waiting for a message. We must take more responsibility with the messages we send them. Children are born loving and accepting, but they must be guided, nurtured, and supported through the modeling and teaching of others. Let's make the choice to actively teach peace, respect, and kindness every day with every child. We can be the generation that makes peace happen.

The violence and hatred of today can be extinguished from our children's tomorrow if we work together teaching the power of peace.

Let's spread this message together. Let's ALL speak peace.

Kate Carroll

Be a peacemaker in your home, school, and community.

Take the Peacemaker Pledge!

I choose kindness over violence.

I choose respect over racism.

I choose empathy over judgment.

I choose knowledge over ignorance.

I choose helping over hurting.

I choose love over hate.

I choose working together instead of against.

I have the choice . . .

I choose peace.

Peace Begins With Me

Words by Kate Carroll

Music by Andrea Carroll

About the Author

Kate Carroll resides in Massachusetts. She has been a first-grade teacher for eleven years and has a master's degree in education. She has a passion for working with children and teaching kindness and peace in her classroom. She strongly believes that with patience, love, and peaceful teaching, we can make this a more peaceful world one child at a time. This is Kate's first published book. For more information on Kate and speaking peace, please visit her website at www.ispeakpeace.com.

About the Illustrator

Rainer M. Osinger is an illustrator, graphic designer, painter, and children's book author. He studied graphics and illustration at (NDC) New Design University in St. Pölten, Austria. He is married and a proud father of seven wonderful children. Rainer lives with his family in St.Veit/Glan Kärnten, Austria. For more information about Rainer and his work, please visit www.osinger-grafik.at.